A Note to Parents and Caregivers:

Read-it! Readers are for children who are just starting on the amazing road to reading. These beautiful books support both the acquisition of reading skills and the love of books.

 The PURPLE LEVEL presents basic topics and objects using high frequency words and simple language patterns.

 The RED LEVEL presents familiar topics using common words and repeating sentence patterns.

 The BLUE LEVEL presents new ideas using a larger vocabulary and varied sentence structure.

 The YELLOW LEVEL presents more challenging ideas, a broad vocabulary, and wide variety in sentence structure.

 The GREEN LEVEL presents more complex ideas, an extended vocabulary range, and expanded language structures.

 The ORANGE LEVEL presents a wide range of ideas and concepts using challenging vocabulary and complex language structures.

When sharing a book with your child, read in short stretches, pausing often to talk about the pictures. Have your child turn the pages and point to the pictures and familiar words. And be sure to reread favorite stories or parts of stories.

There is no right or wrong way to share books with children. Find time to read with your child, and pass on the legacy of literacy.

Adria F. Klein, Ph.D.
Professor Emeritus
California State University
San Bernardino, California

Editor: Christianne Jones
Designer: Tracy Kaehler
Page Production: Lori Bye
Creative Director: Keith Griffin
Editorial Director: Carol Jones
The illustrations in this book were created with acrylics.

Picture Window Books
5115 Excelsior Boulevard
Suite 232
Minneapolis, MN 55416
877-845-8392
www.picturewindowbooks.com

Printed in the United States of America.

Library of Congress Cataloging-in-Publication Data
Donahue, Jill L.
Danny's birthday / by Jill L. Donahue ; illustrated by Ronnie Rooney.
p. cm. — (Read-it! readers)
Summary: Danny has a wonderful time opening presents on his birthday.
ISBN-13: 978-1-4048-2408-9 (hardcover)
ISBN-10: 1-4048-2408-1 (hardcover)
[1. Birthdays—Fiction. 2. Gifts—Fiction.] I. Rooney, Ronnie, ill. II. Title. III. Series.

PZ8.3.D7234Dan 2006
[E]—dc22   2006003425

Danny's Birthday

by Jill L. Donahue
illustrated by Ronnie Rooney

Special thanks to our advisers for their expertise:

Adria F. Klein, Ph.D.
Professor Emeritus, California State University
San Bernardino, California

Susan Kesselring, M.A.
Literacy Educator
Rosemount–Apple Valley–Eagan (Minnesota) School District

PiCTURE WiNDOW BOOKS
Minneapolis, Minnesota

It's Danny's birthday. He is six years old today. He gets lots of presents and is ready to play!

5

He gets a balloon with a big
yellow star.

He gets a toy truck that can go really far.

9

He gets a stuffed camel with a large hump.

He gets three spotted frogs that love to jump.

He gets a baseball to use at the park.

He gets a loud puppy that likes
to bark.

He gets new paints that are blue, green, and red.

He gets a bright light to put by
his bed.

21

The presents are great, and so is the cake. But look at the mess that Danny creates!

More *Read-it!* Readers

Bright pictures and fun stories help you practice your reading skills. Look for more books at your level.

Back to School 1-4048-1166-4
The Bath 1-4048-1576-7
The Best Snowman 1-4048-0048-4
Bill's Baggy Pants 1-4048-0050-6
Camping Trip 1-4048-1167-2
Days of the Week 1-4048-1581-3
Eric Won't Do It 1-4048-1188-5
Fable's Whistle 1-4048-1169-9
Finny Learns to Swim 1-4048-1582-1
Goldie's New Home 1-4048-1171-0
I Am in Charge of Me 1-4048-0646-6
The Lazy Scarecrow 1-4048-0062-X
Little Joe's Big Race 1-4048-0063-8
The Little Star 1-4048-0065-4
Meg Takes a Walk 1-4048-1005-6
The Naughty Puppy 1-4048-0067-0
Paula's Letter 1-4048-1183-4
Selfish Sophie 1-4048-0069-7
The Tall, Tall Slide 1-4048-1186-9
The Traveling Shoes 1-4048-1588-0
A Trip to the Zoo 1-4048-1590-2
Willy the Worm 1-4048-1593-7

Looking for a specific title or level? A complete list of *Read-it!* Readers is available on our Web site:
www.picturewindowbooks.com